Let's Draw
Bible Heroes

Written by Anita Ganeri
Illustrated by Rachel Conner

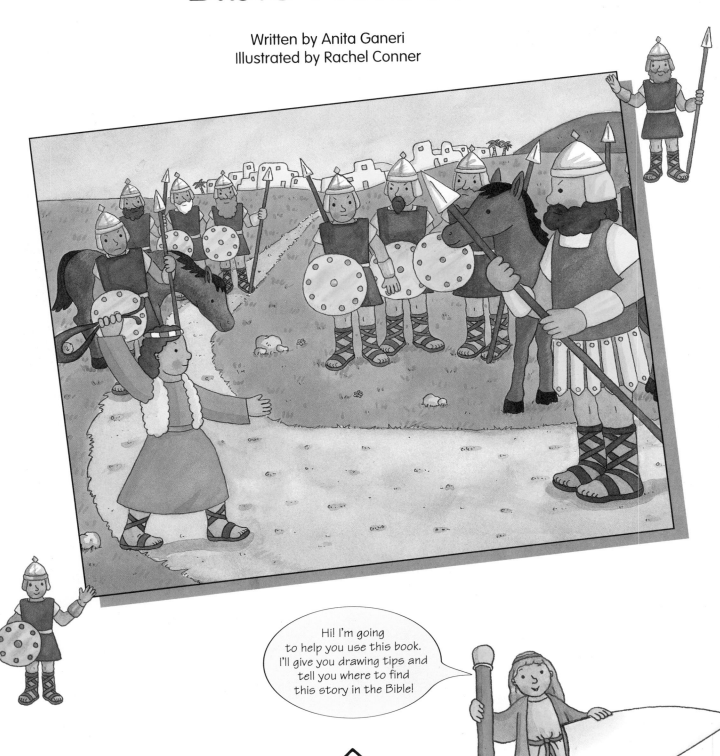

Hi! I'm going
to help you use this book.
I'll give you drawing tips and
tell you where to find
this story in the Bible!

RANDOM HOUSE

GETTING STARTED

Have you always wished you could draw but never known where to begin? Then look no further! This is the book for you. In it, you can find out how to draw the stories of Bible heroes.

Below are some of the things you may need to get started. Before you begin, let's make sure you have everything you need.

Look in the back of the book for your grid pages.

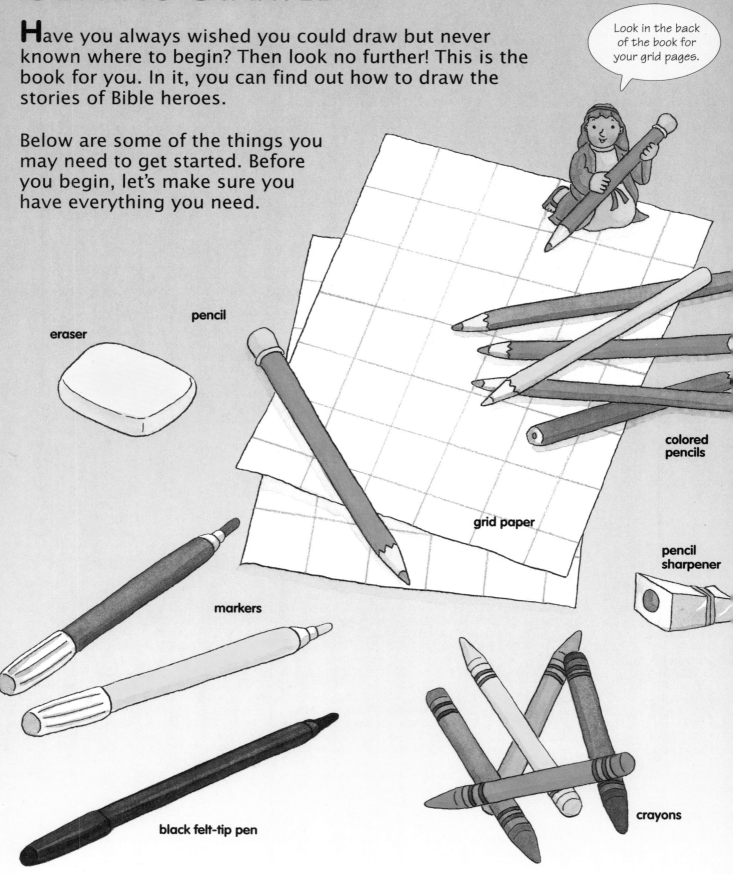

eraser

pencil

colored pencils

grid paper

pencil sharpener

markers

crayons

black felt-tip pen

USING THE GRIDS

At the back of this book, you'll find some grid pages. They'll help you to follow the drawing steps by showing you exactly where to add each new line. Pull them out carefully. If you run out of grids, ask a grown-up to help you photocopy or draw some more.

1 & **2** Copy each drawing, step by step, onto your grid paper, noticing where the drawing should touch the lines on your grid. Draw lightly in pencil first. Each new step appears in blue to show you exactly what to draw next.

3 When you have finished, go over the lines you want to keep in felt-tip pen and erase any leftover pencil lines.

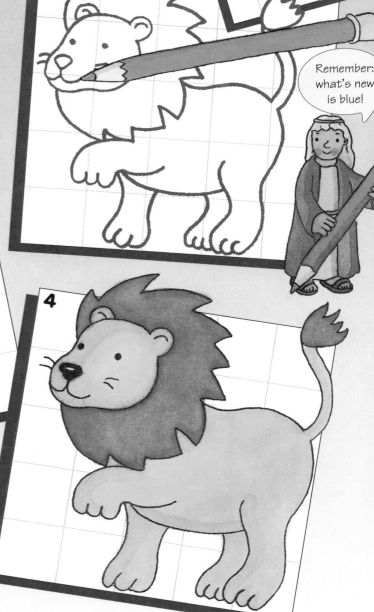

Remember: what's new is blue!

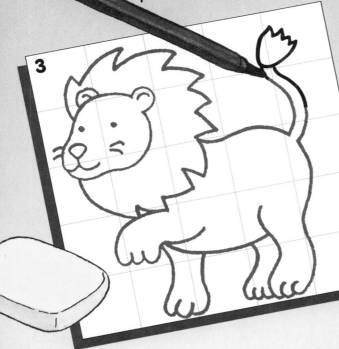

4 Congratulations! Now you have a finished drawing! You can fill in your picture using your colored pencils or crayons. The final step of each drawing is shown in full color – so you can copy it. You'll also find some coloring tips on page 24.

JONAH AND THE WHALE

God told Jonah to go to Nineveh and warn the people to stop doing bad things. But Jonah ran away to sea instead. A terrible storm hit. The boat was battered by wind and waves. Jonah knew God had sent the storm. He told the sailors to throw him overboard. When they did, the storm stopped!

A gigantic creature, probably a whale, swam by and rescued Jonah by swallowing him. Jonah prayed that God would forgive him. God heard his prayers, and the whale put Jonah onto dry land, safe and sound. This time Jonah did as God said and went to Nineveh.

You can read about Jonah and the whale in the book of Jonah.

When you have learned to draw the characters and animals in this book, try drawing this scene of Jonah and the whale.

Fish

Shell

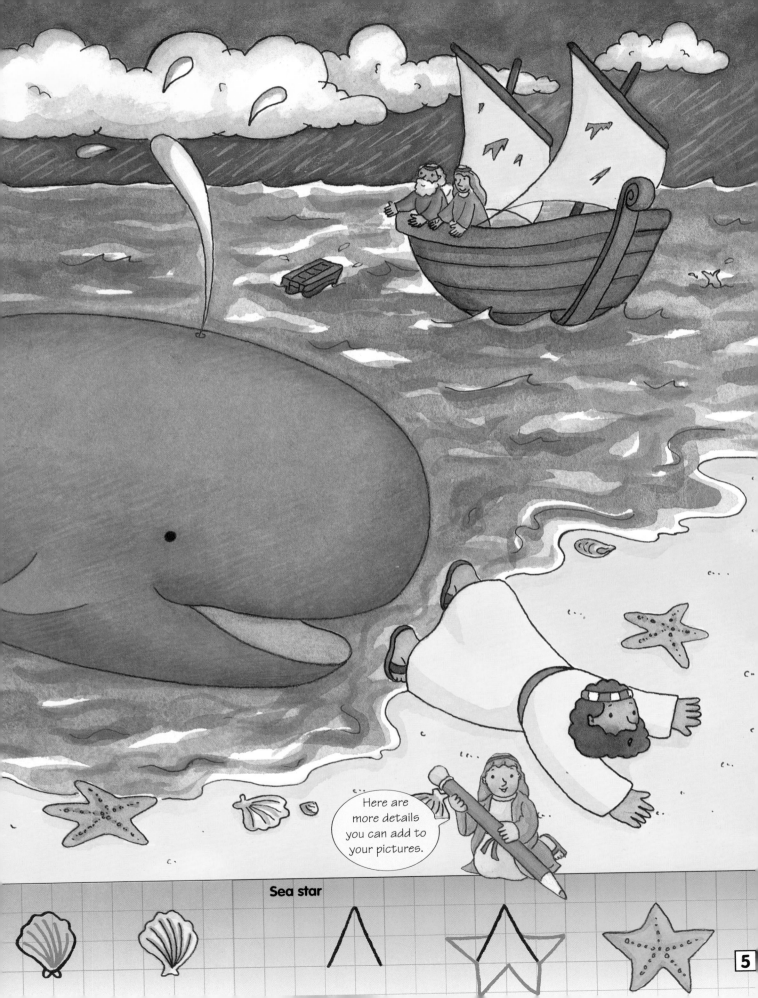

Here are more details you can add to your pictures.

Sea star

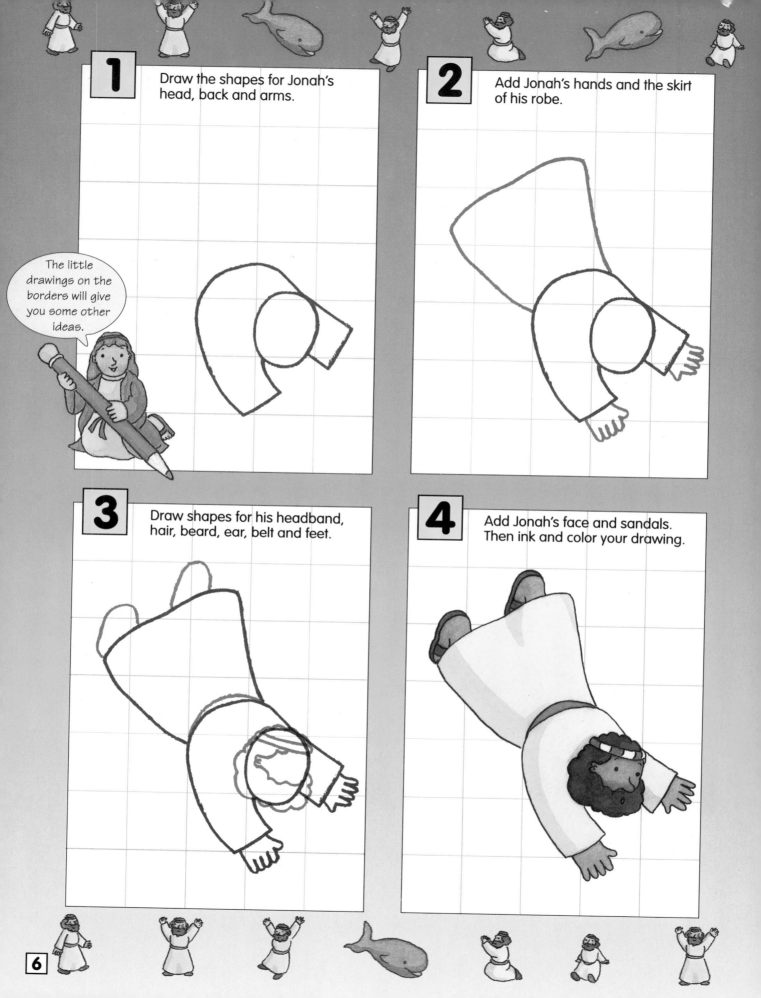

1 Draw the shapes for Jonah's head, back and arms.

2 Add Jonah's hands and the skirt of his robe.

The little drawings on the borders will give you some other ideas.

3 Draw shapes for his headband, hair, beard, ear, belt and feet.

4 Add Jonah's face and sandals. Then ink and color your drawing.

1 Draw a large teardrop shape for the whale's body.

2 Add two smaller leaf shapes for its flukes.

Remember to erase your leftover pencil lines before you color.

3 Draw an eye and a flipper, and the shape of an open mouth.

4 Finish the mouth and add a waterspout.

Then ink and color your drawing.

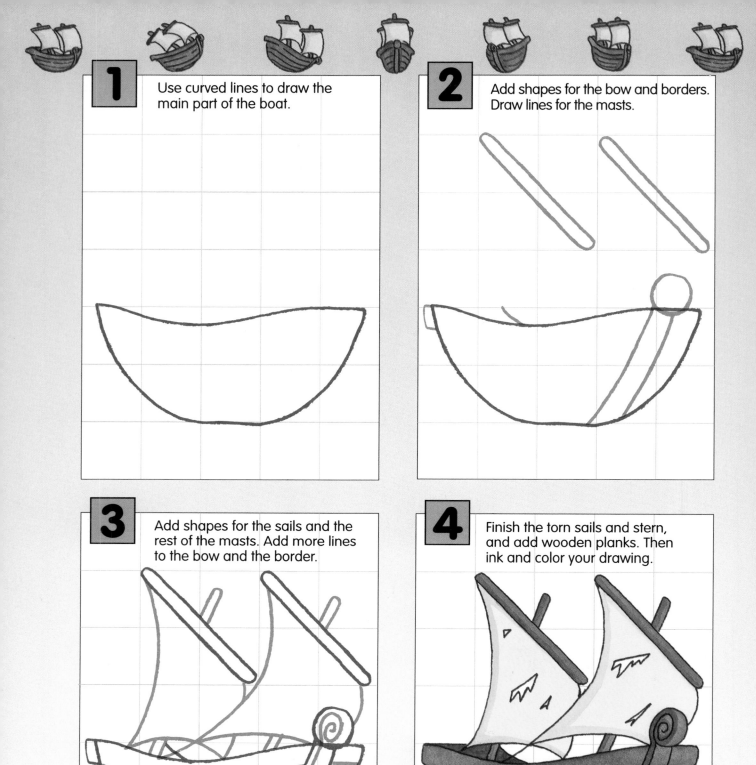

1 Use curved lines to draw the main part of the boat.

2 Add shapes for the bow and borders. Draw lines for the masts.

3 Add shapes for the sails and the rest of the masts. Add more lines to the bow and the border.

4 Finish the torn sails and stern, and add wooden planks. Then ink and color your drawing.

ACTION

Now that you have learned to draw a boat and a whale, try making them move. To do this, you need to change their positions. You can see how to do this in the pictures below.

Start with the boat position you learned how to draw on page 8. Using the same shapes for the main part of the boat and sails, make the boat lean backward as if it is heaving and rolling on the waves.

Remember to look at the borders for even more action ideas!

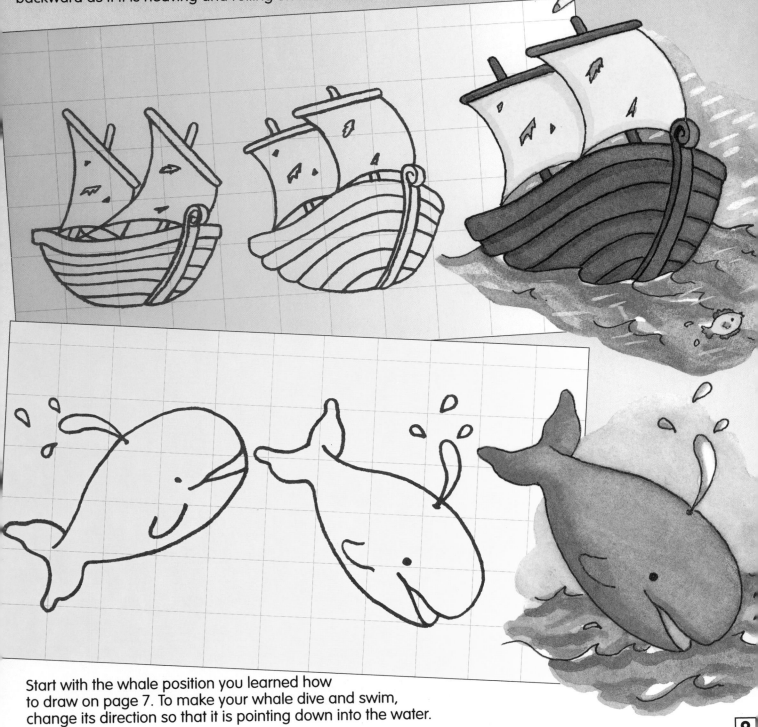

Start with the whale position you learned how to draw on page 7. To make your whale dive and swim, change its direction so that it is pointing down into the water.

DANIEL IN THE LIONS' DEN

Daniel was a good worker, so the king gave him a high position in his kingdom. The other officials were jealous. They tricked the king into making a law. Every man was to worship the king only. Daniel loved and worshiped only God. The king had to throw Daniel into the lions' den. In the morning, he found Daniel alive and well with the lions. God had sent an angel to protect him from the lions' strong jaws. The king was happy, and ordered everyone in his whole kingdom to worship Daniel's God.

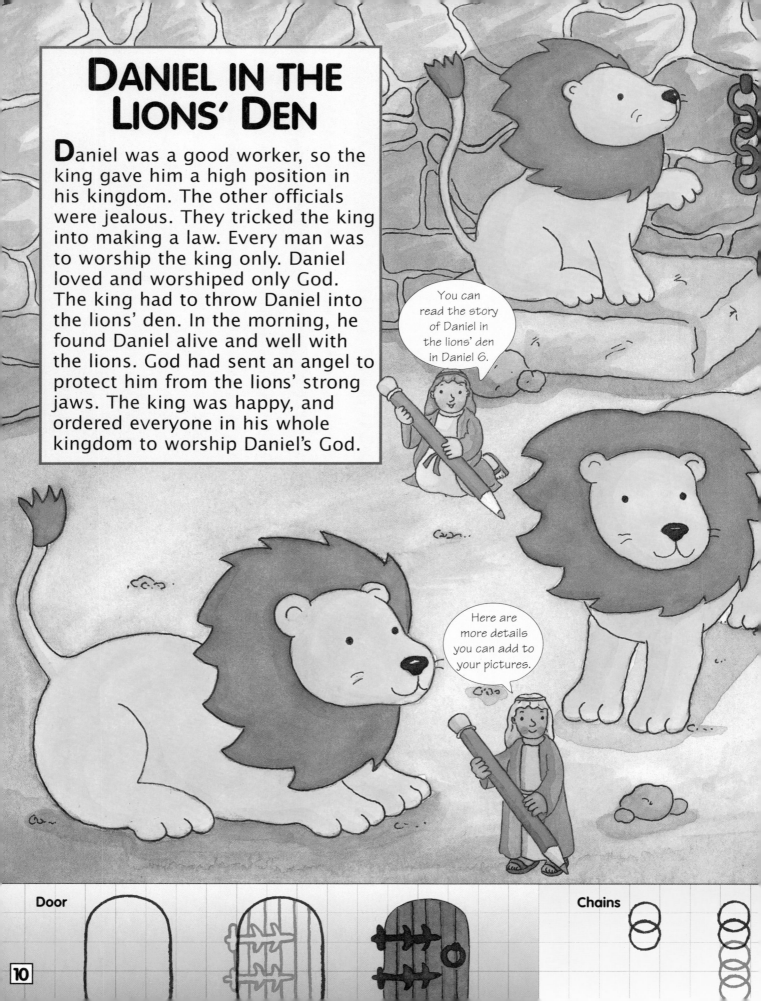

Door

Chains

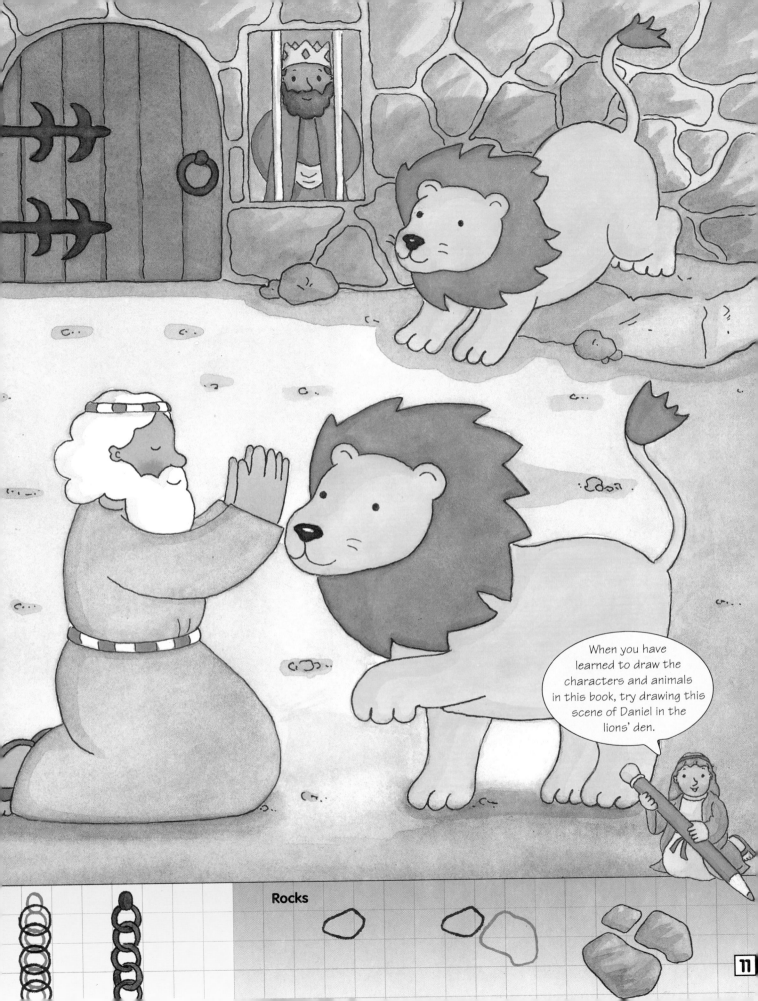

When you have learned to draw the characters and animals in this book, try drawing this scene of Daniel in the lions' den.

Rocks

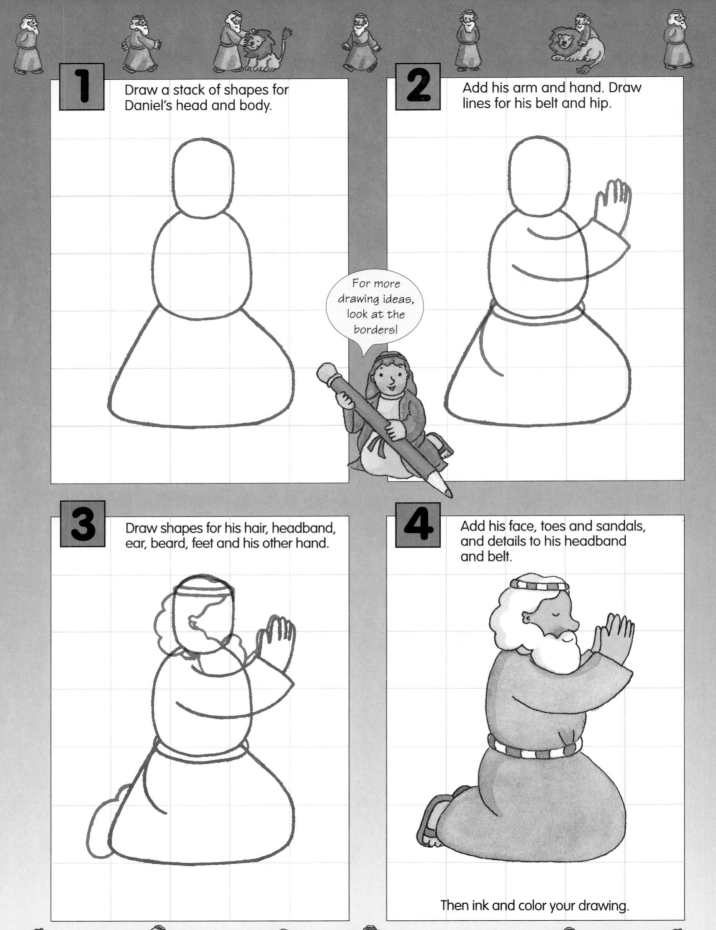

1 Draw a stack of shapes for Daniel's head and body.

2 Add his arm and hand. Draw lines for his belt and hip.

For more drawing ideas, look at the borders!

3 Draw shapes for his hair, headband, ear, beard, feet and his other hand.

4 Add his face, toes and sandals, and details to his headband and belt.

Then ink and color your drawing.

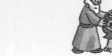

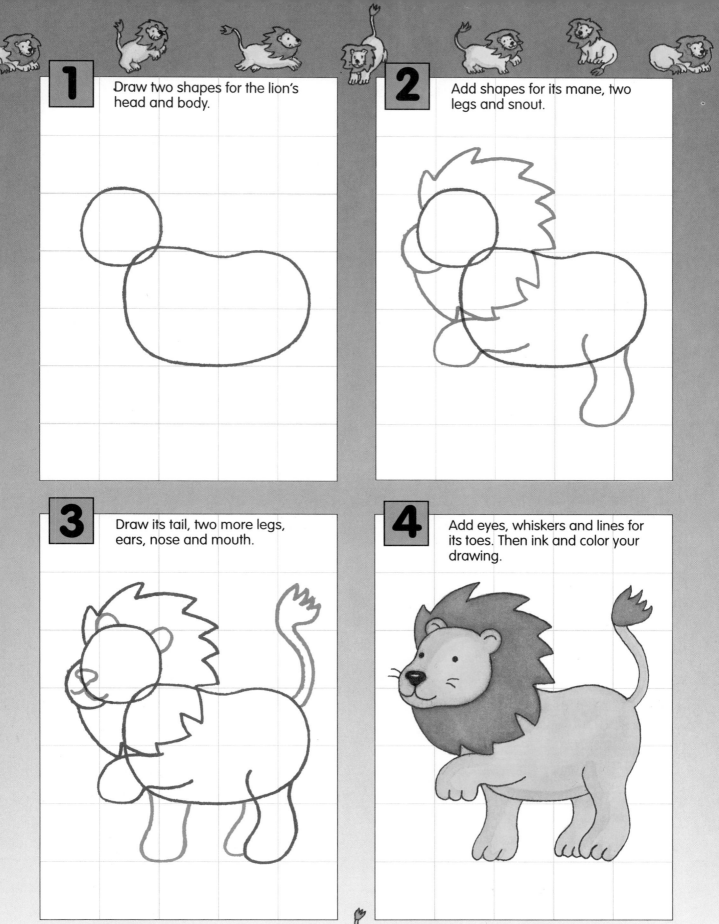

1 Draw two shapes for the lion's head and body.

2 Add shapes for its mane, two legs and snout.

3 Draw its tail, two more legs, ears, nose and mouth.

4 Add eyes, whiskers and lines for its toes. Then ink and color your drawing.

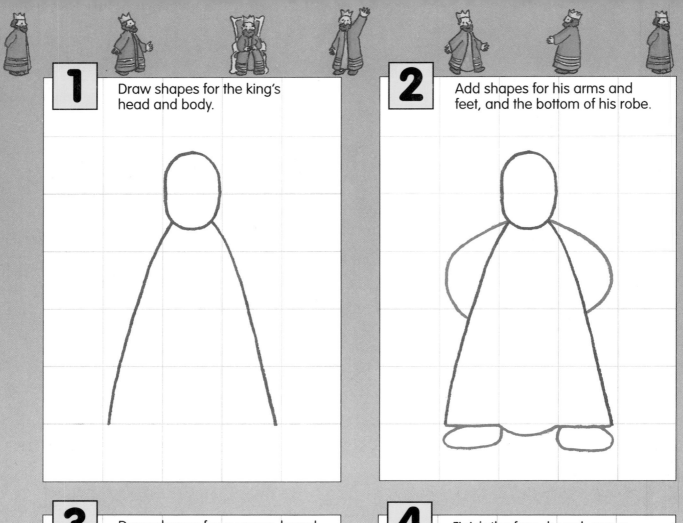

1
Draw shapes for the king's head and body.

2
Add shapes for his arms and feet, and the bottom of his robe.

3
Draw shapes for a crown, beard, ears, clothes and shoes.

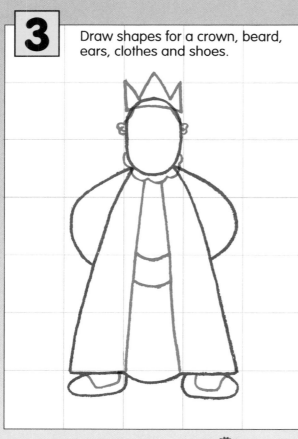

4
Finish the face, beard, crown, clothes and shoes.

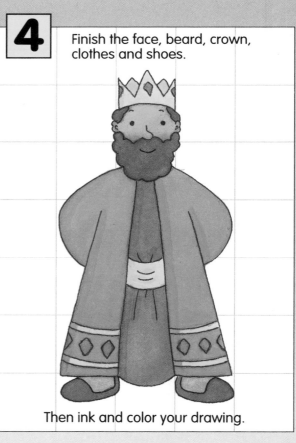

Then ink and color your drawing.

ACTION

Now that you have learned to draw some of the characters in the story of Daniel in the lions' den, try making them move. To do this, you need to change the position of their bodies and legs. You can see how to do this in the pictures shown here.

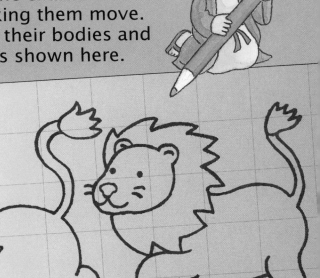

Remember to look at the borders for even more action ideas.

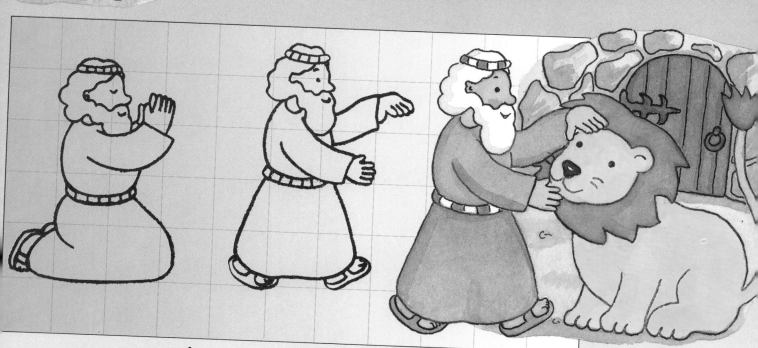

Start with the lion position you learned how to draw on page 13. Stretch out its front and back legs to make it leap.

Start with the position of Daniel kneeling, which you learned how to draw on page 12. Stretch out his legs and lower his arms to make Daniel stand.

DAVID AND GOLIATH

The Israelites and Philistines were getting ready to fight each other. David's father sent him with food for his brothers in the Israelite army. As he approached, little David saw the giant Goliath challenging any Israelite to fight him. Whoever beat him would win the battle. "I will fight him," said David. "God will protect me."

Goliath laughed when he saw David. But David then put one small stone in his sling and hurled it at the giant. It hit the giant in the middle of his forehead and killed him. Little David had defeated the giant Goliath with the help of one small stone – and a great God!

You can read the story of David and Goliath in I Samuel 17.

When you have learned to draw the characters and animals in this book, try drawing this scene of David and Goliath.

Shield

Tree

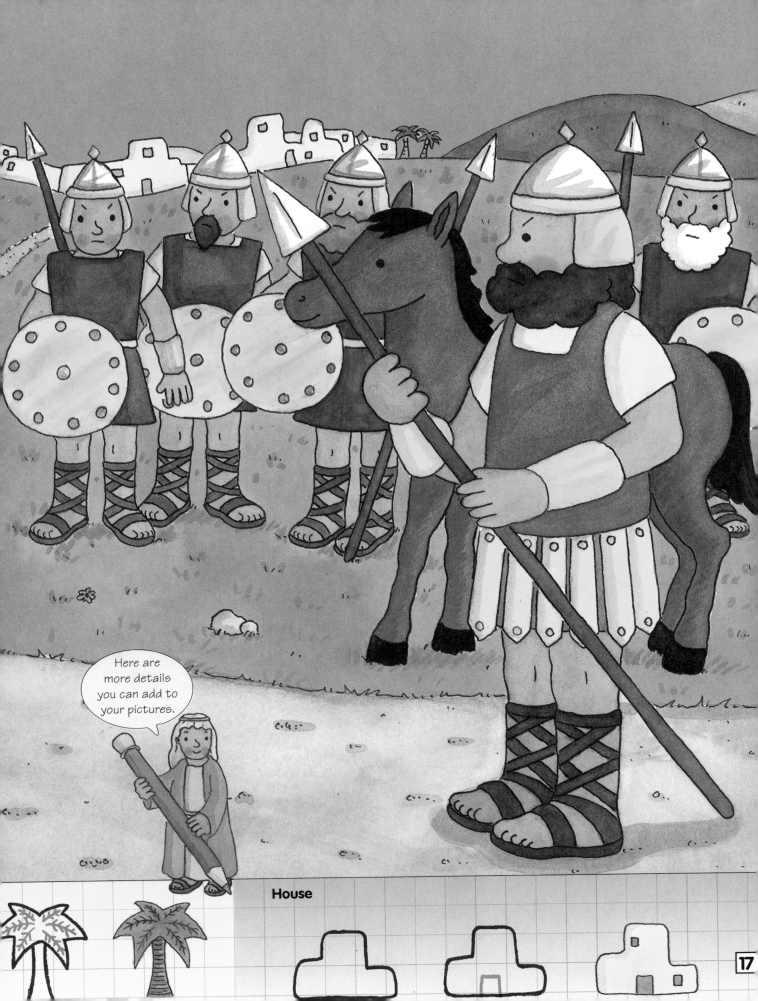

House

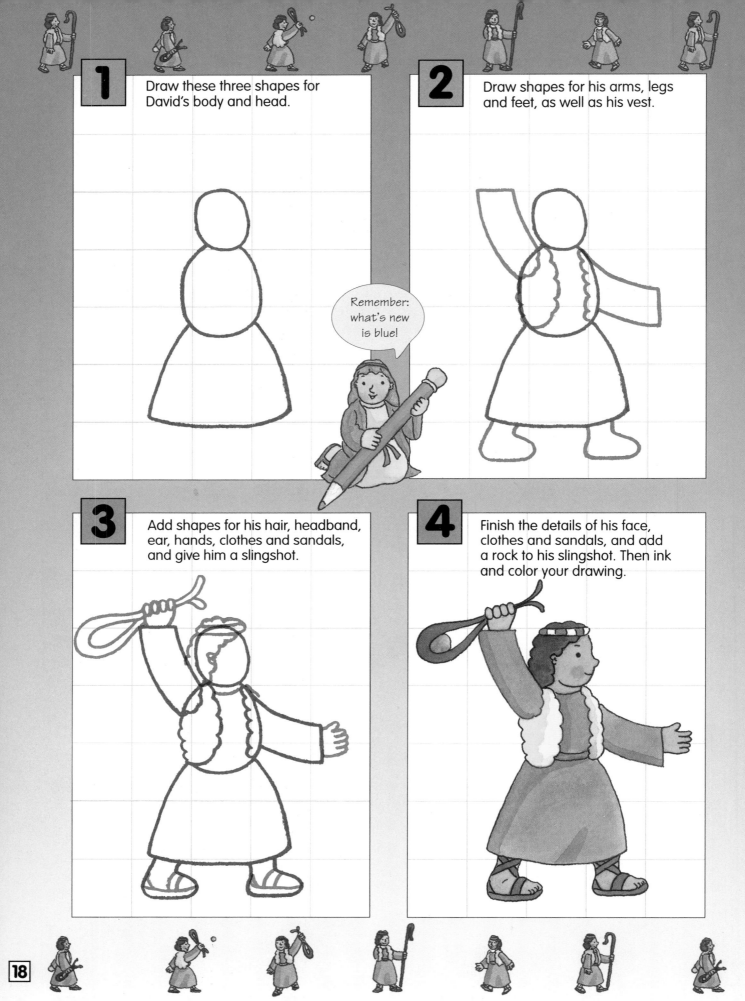

1 Draw these three shapes for David's body and head.

2 Draw shapes for his arms, legs and feet, as well as his vest.

Remember: what's new is blue!

3 Add shapes for his hair, headband, ear, hands, clothes and sandals, and give him a slingshot.

4 Finish the details of his face, clothes and sandals, and add a rock to his slingshot. Then ink and color your drawing.

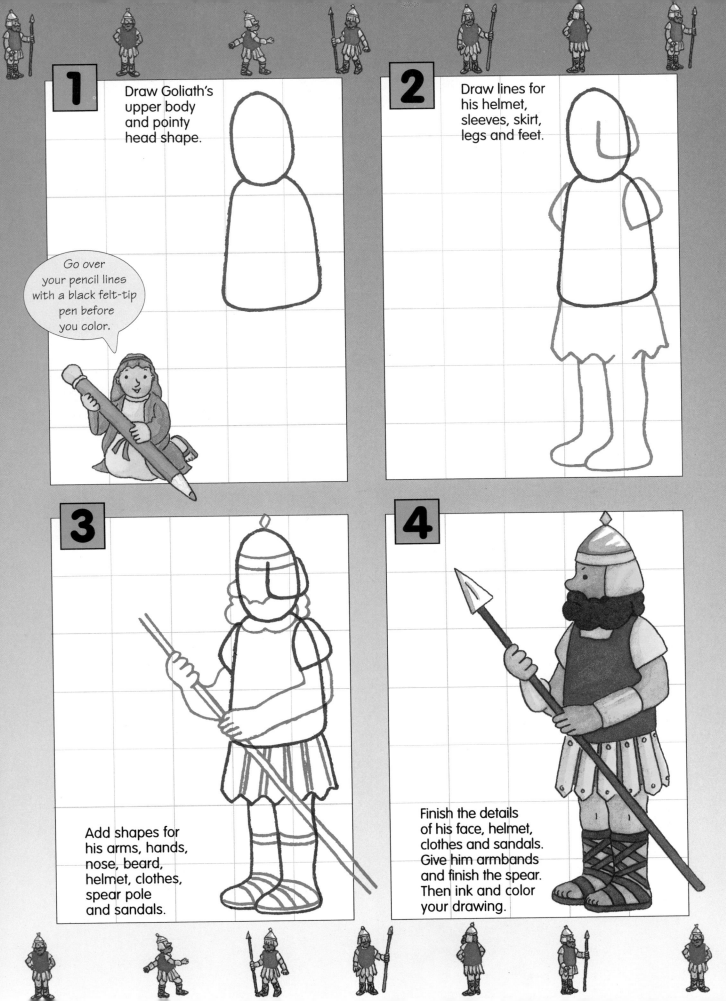

1 Draw Goliath's upper body and pointy head shape.

Go over your pencil lines with a black felt-tip pen before you color.

2 Draw lines for his helmet, sleeves, skirt, legs and feet.

3 Add shapes for his arms, hands, nose, beard, helmet, clothes, spear pole and sandals.

4 Finish the details of his face, helmet, clothes and sandals. Give him armbands and finish the spear. Then ink and color your drawing.

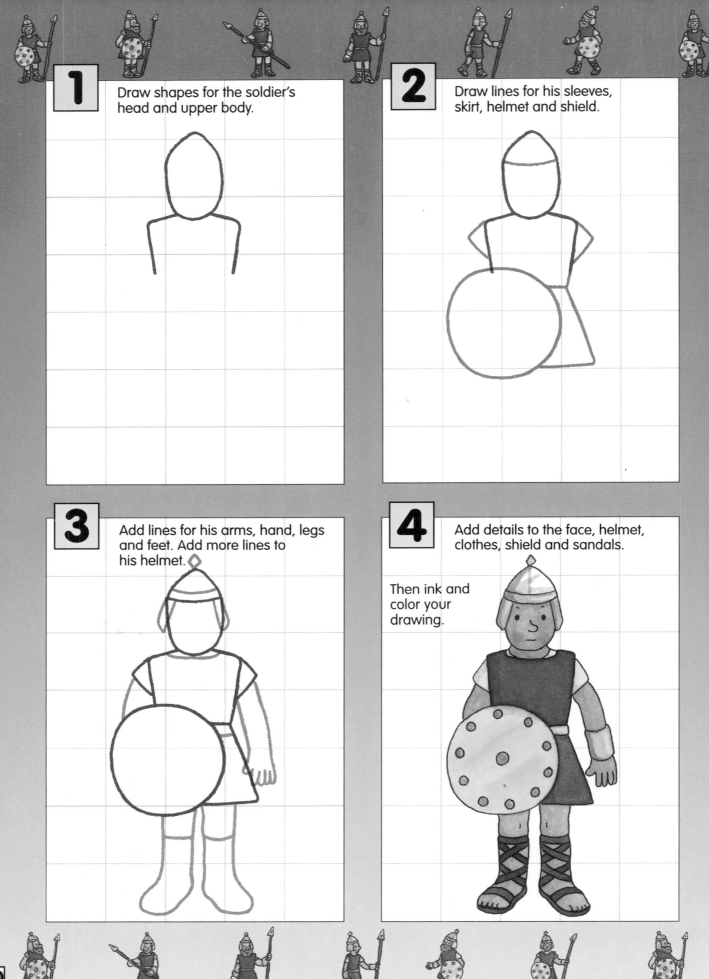

1 Draw shapes for the soldier's head and upper body.

2 Draw lines for his sleeves, skirt, helmet and shield.

3 Add lines for his arms, hand, legs and feet. Add more lines to his helmet.

4 Add details to the face, helmet, clothes, shield and sandals.

Then ink and color your drawing.

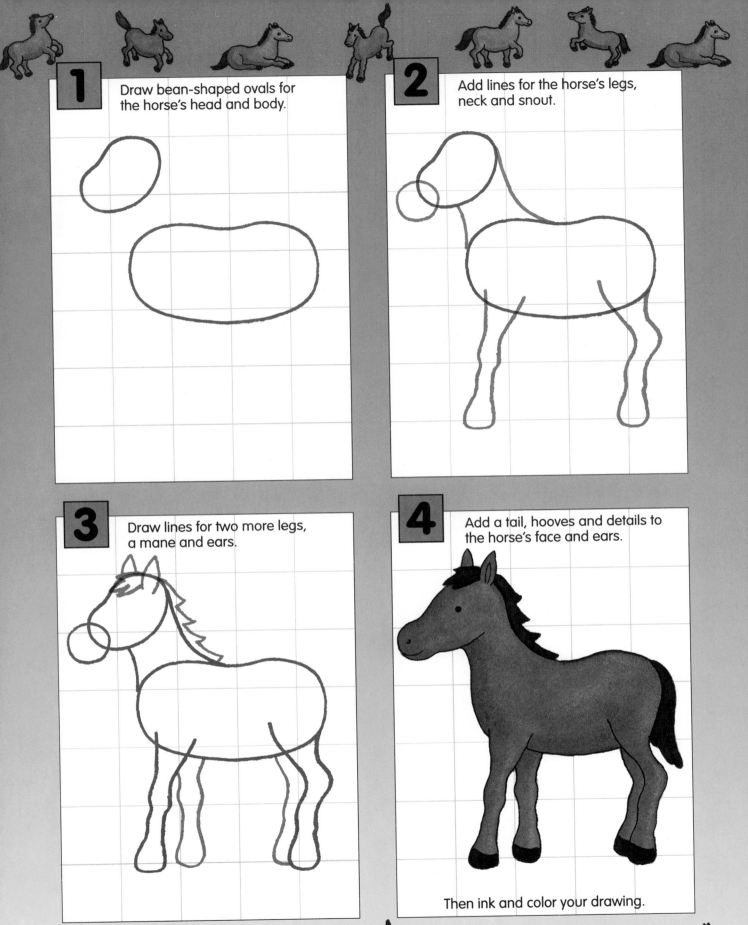

1 Draw bean-shaped ovals for the horse's head and body.

2 Add lines for the horse's legs, neck and snout.

3 Draw lines for two more legs, a mane and ears.

4 Add a tail, hooves and details to the horse's face and ears.

Then ink and color your drawing.

ACTION

Now that you have learned to draw some of the characters in the story of David and Goliath, try making them move. To do this, you need to change their shapes and positions. You can see how to do this in the pictures shown here.

Remember to look back at the borders for even more action ideas!

Start with the position of David you learned how to draw on page 18. Move the arm and slingshot in front to make David swing the slingshot.

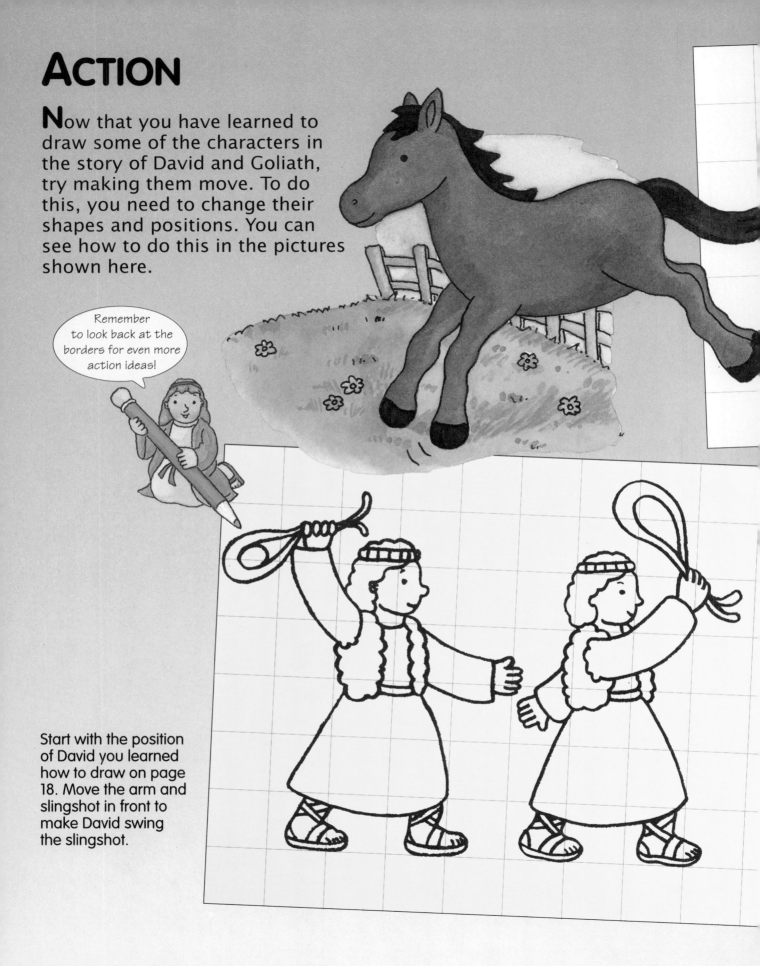

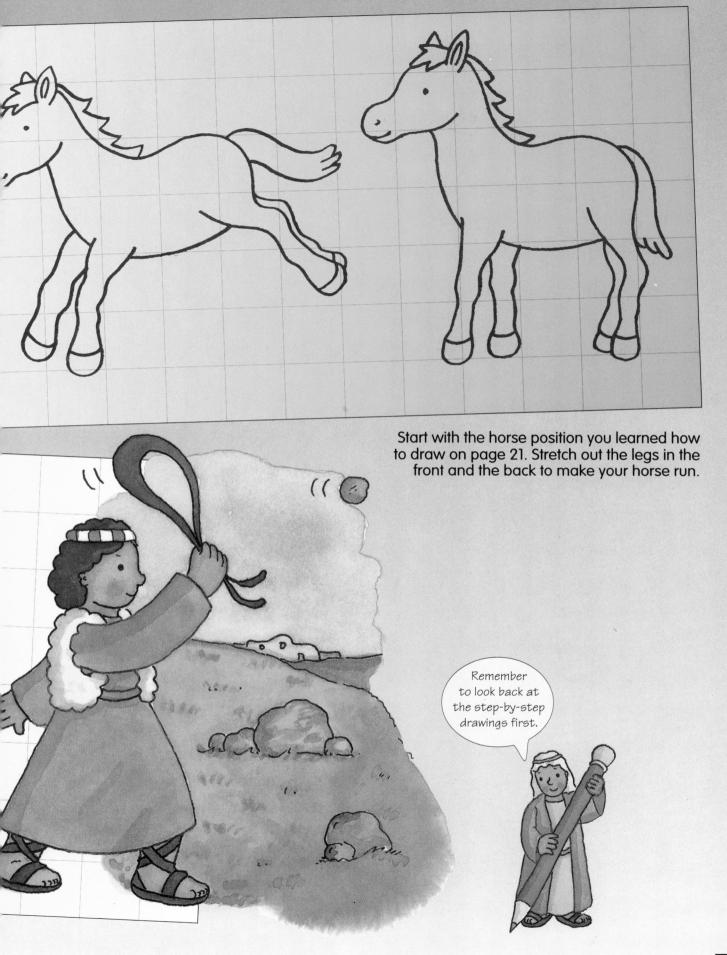

Start with the horse position you learned how to draw on page 21. Stretch out the legs in the front and the back to make your horse run.

Remember to look back at the step-by-step drawings first.

COLORING YOUR DRAWINGS

When you've finished the outlines of each of your drawings, have fun coloring them. Here are some tips on ways to color.

You can try different color paper, too! Try rough paper or smooth paper for different textures!

Markers:
Use these to get a smooth, even finish. Also, by placing your marker at different angles, you can make thin or thick lines.

Colored Pencils:
These are good to use if you want the texture of the paper to show through.

Crayons:
You can blend different colors of crayons together to make a totally new color.

Use the following grid pages for your drawings. Don't forget to mak photocopies!

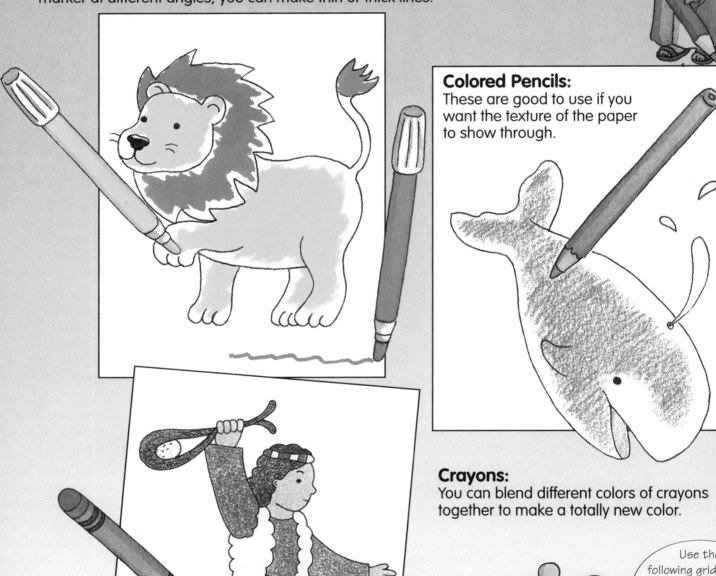